Make a Masterpiece

Colored Pencils

by Alix Wood

Gareth Stevens
PUBLISHING

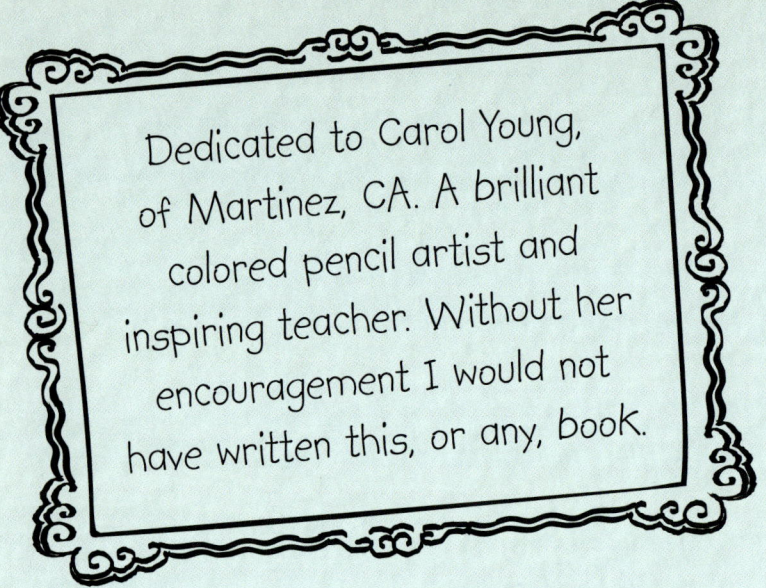

Dedicated to Carol Young, of Martinez, CA. A brilliant colored pencil artist and inspiring teacher. Without her encouragement I would not have written this, or any, book.

Please visit our website, www.garethstevens.com. For a free color catalog of all our high-quality books, call toll free 1-800-542-2595 or fax 1-877-542-2596.

Cataloging-in-Publication Data

Names: Wood, Alix.
Title: Colored pencils / Alix Wood.
Description: New York : Gareth Stevens Publishing, 2019. | Series: Make a masterpiece | Includes glossary and index.
Identifiers: ISBN 9781538235829 (pbk.) | ISBN 9781538235942 (library bound) | ISBN 9781538235867 (6pack)
Subjects: LCSH: Colored pencil drawing--Technique--Juvenile literature.
Classification: LCC NC892.W66 2019 | DDC 741.2'4--dc23

First Edition

Published in 2019 by
Gareth Stevens Publishing
111 East 14th Street, Suite 349
New York, NY 10003

© Alix Wood Books

Produced for Gareth Stevens by Alix Wood Books
Designed by Alix Wood
Editor: Eloise Macgregor

Photo credits:
Cover and title page background, 3 background, 4 top, 5, 6, 7 top, 11 top © Adobe Stock Images; 7 bottom © Michael Maggs; all other images © Alix Wood

Printed in the United States of America

CPSIA compliance information: Batch #CW19GS For further information contact Gareth Stevens, New York, New York at 1-800-542-2595.

Contents

Using Colored Pencils

Most people have tried drawing with colored pencils at some point. They are great to use when you are learning to draw, and they can also be used to create some really amazing art. Their sharp point means you can draw fine detail. You can use them lightly for a soft look, or press hard and build up **layers** for a strong look. Colored pencils are also really easy to carry around, and you don't need to wait for them to dry!

There are three main types of colored pencils: wax-based, oil-based, and watercolor pencils. Wax-based pencils are soft and a little easier to erase than the others. Oil-based pencils create a strong color and are harder, so they stay sharp longer. Watercolor pencils can be blended with water and a brush.

This drawing was created by the author using wax-based colored pencils.

What Will You Need?

Colored Pencils

Most projects in this book can be done using good quality wax-based colored pencils. They are not too expensive to buy. You will definitely need a black, white, red, blue, and yellow. A 24-color set is about perfect. Don't worry that you don't have every color. You can mix new colors by layering them over each other.

Paper

You can either use a smooth paper, or a paper with a small amount of **texture**. The texture helps hold each color on the paper as you build up layers of pencil. A medium-weight paper is best. If your paper is too thin, it won't be able to hold much color. You can use white or colored paper.

A Good Pencil Sharpener

Use a sharpener with a reasonably new, sharp blade. Wax-based pencils can break easily. You will need to sharpen your pencils quite often, especially if you want a fine point.

Eraser

You can't erase colored pencil marks completely, but you can lighten them. A kneaded eraser is great for cleaning up pencil crumbs, too.

You will also need a pencil, ruler, lip balm, a tissue, some paintbrushes, an ink pen, and ocher acrylic paint.

All About Pencils

Once you have your set of colored pencils, it is important to look after them. Their soft **core** can break easily. There are several tips you can learn to help keep your pencils from breaking.

Keep your pencils in a container. If you always put each pencil back in the container, they won't roll off the table and break. If you transport your pencils, put them in a padded pencil case. You can easily make your own pencil wrap, too. Cut a piece of cloth or bubble wrap large enough to go around your pencils. Then fasten your wrap together using a rubber band or some string.

TIP

If the core of one of your pencils does break, it may not mean the end for your pencil. Try this tip to fix it again. Place your pencil in a warm spot, such as on a windowsill on a hot day. The heat will soften the wax in the pencil, and cause the broken core to melt together again!

How to Sharpen Your Pencils

1 Check that your sharpener blade is sharp enough. If it produces a long shaving, it is in good condition. If it cuts off little pieces instead, your sharpener is too blunt or the blade is too loose.

2 Ask an adult to tighten the small screw in your sharpener. If that doesn't improve the sharpener, ask an adult to replace the blade, or find another sharpener.

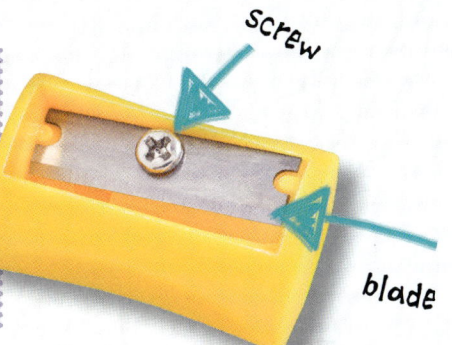

screw

blade

3 Hold your pencil in one hand and the sharpener in the other. Gently turn the pencil sharpener while holding the pencil still.

Master Class

Using a Color Wheel

A color wheel (right) is a useful tool to help work out what colors will go well together, or will **contrast** well. Opposite colors on the wheel provide a good contrast, so a red will stand out well against a green, for example. Colors next to each other on the wheel will look good together.

Shading and Texture

Try some of these ways to add **shading** and texture to your colored pencil drawing. Draw five circles on some paper. Decide where you want your light to come from. The side opposite the light will be in shadow. Then, shade each circle a different way.

Hatching

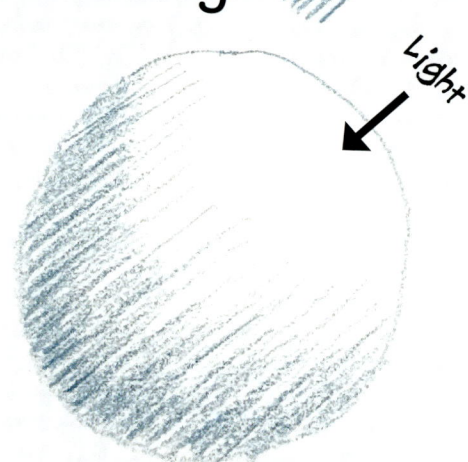

Hatching uses lines going in the same direction to shade an object. The closer the lines, the darker that area will appear.

Crosshatching

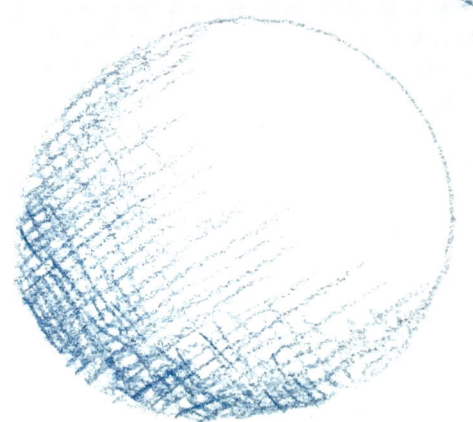

Crosshatching uses hatching lines and then another set of lines that cross at **right angles**.

Using Dots

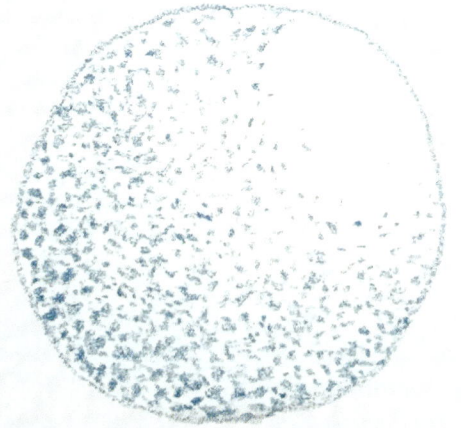

Using dots to shade your picture is called **stippling**. The closer together the dots are, the darker that area will look.

Curved Lines

You can also shade a circle by drawing lines that follow the curve of the circle. Add more lines to create darker shadows.

8

Scumbling

Scumbling uses random squiggles as a shading technique. The more you overlap the squiggles, the darker that area will look.

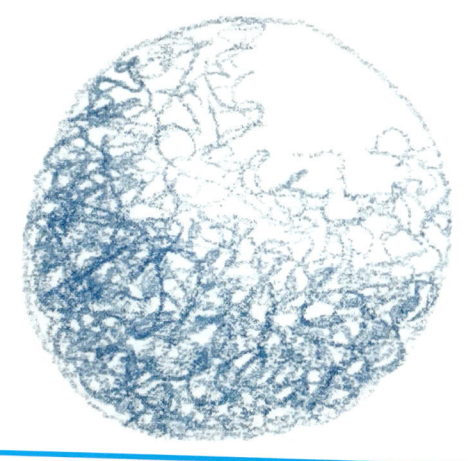

Master Class

Pencil Pressure

If you change how hard you press with your pencil you can change how light or dark your shading is, too. Try shading some squares by simply moving your pencil back and forth. Gradually increase the amount of pressure you use for each square. The harder you press, the darker your shade will be.

See if you can create one long **graded** rectangle moving from heavy pressure to light pressure.

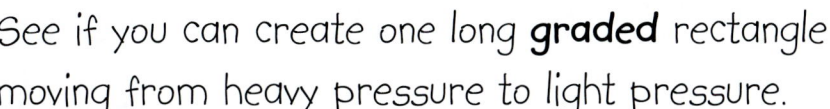

Now try **blending** two colors. Create a graded rectangle in one color. Then turn your paper upside down and draw another graded rectangle on top using a different color.

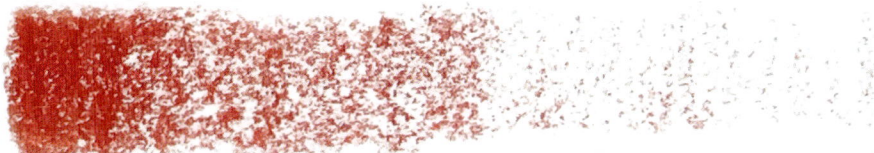

Underpainting

Instead of using different shades of green to color in this apple, we used a technique known as **underpainting**. With underpainting, you shade the object first using a single color pencil. Then you can simply go over the shading you have done using the object's color.

Draw a simple apple shape using a regular lead pencil.

Shade your apple using the same lead pencil.

Go over the apple using green pencil. The shading can be seen through the green layer.

Leave a white **highlight** where the light hits the apple.

You can add some yellows and reds to your apple, too. Perhaps put a touch of brown on the stalk.

TIP

Another great way to shade an object is to use the color that is opposite it on the color wheel (see page 7). So, to shade a green apple, you could do your underpainting using a red pencil.

Master Class

Color a Photocopy

Choose a picture and make a *black* and *white* print or photocopy of it.

When you color over the photocopy using colored pencil, the shading will show through like an underpainting.

We colored our car red, and added a tint of blue to the windows and hubcaps. We added a dash of yellow to the headlights. We also left some areas white, where the light would be hitting the car.

Op Art Hand

Op art is short for **optical illusion** art. An optical illusion is something that tricks your eyes and makes you think you *see* something that is not really there. Use shading to create this ghostly hand! You will need an ink pen or fine permanent marker for this project. Don't use a ballpoint as it may smudge.

1

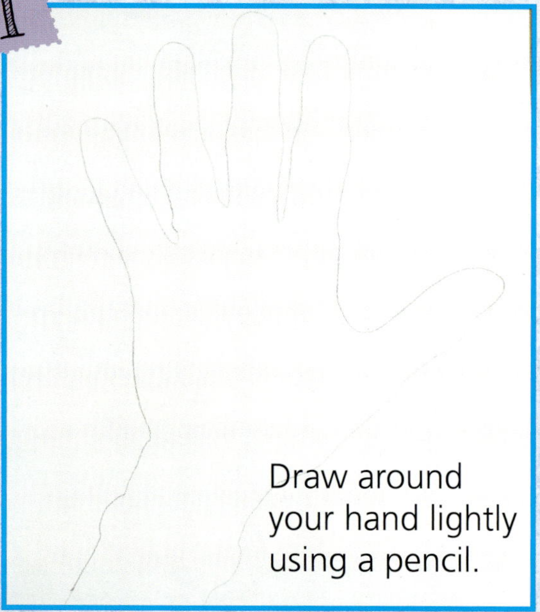

Draw around your hand lightly using a pencil.

2

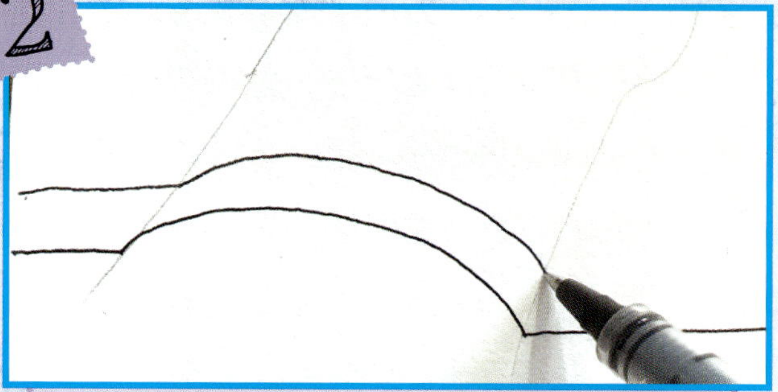

Draw straight lines across your paper, but when you reach any part of your hand outline, draw an **arc** shape. At the other side of your hand, draw straight lines again to the edge of the paper.

3

Continue up your hand, drawing arcs over each finger and thumb.

4

Now add your color shading to create your optical illusion effect. Use heavy pressure at each side of every arc to create darker, shadowed areas.

5

Leave a white highlight down the center of each arc. Use lighter pressure on the remaining arc and straight line. Your hand will start to pop out of the paper!

Mixing, Shading, and Blending

Color Mixing

The shading techniques that you practiced on pages 8 and 9 can be used to mix colors, too. Try it.

To make a green color, put layers of yellow and blue crosshatching on top of each other.

To make a purple, stipple an area with red and blue dots.

To mix an orange, scumble an area using red and yellow squiggles.

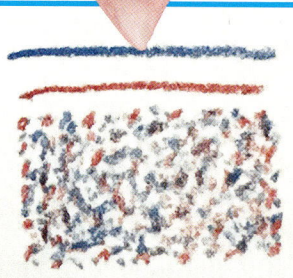

Different Ways of Shading

You can add shade to an object in a few ways. You can use a darker shade of the object's color. You can use black. Or, remember the color wheel on page 7? You can use the color opposite it on the color wheel, known as its **complementary** color, which creates a richer shadow.

This ball is drawn and shaded using one color, green.

This ball is drawn in green, with shading done using black pencil.

Here is another green ball shaded using its complementary color, red.

Blending Colored Pencils

One of the best things about wax-based colored pencils is that you can blend them to create a nice glassy surface. Try your hand at blending with this simple flower design.

1

Draw a simple flower outline using purple colored pencil.

2

Shade the tip and base of each petal, leaving the middle section as a highlight.

3

Repeat step 2 until you have colored in all the petals.

4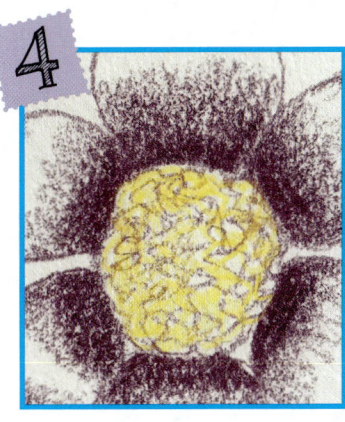

Scumble the center of the flower using yellow and purple pencil.

5

To blend your petals, take a white pencil. Starting with the lightest areas, color over the purple.

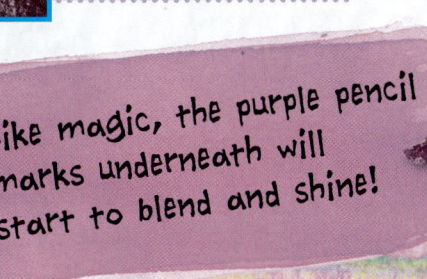

Like magic, the purple pencil marks underneath will start to blend and shine!

Blended Lines

You can use lip balm to make your pencils blend as you draw! Try this op art project and see how it works. You will need an ink pen or fine permanent marker to draw your outlines. Don't use a ballpoint as it may smudge.

1

Using an ink pen, draw some random squiggly lines down the page. Make sure that none of them overlap.

2

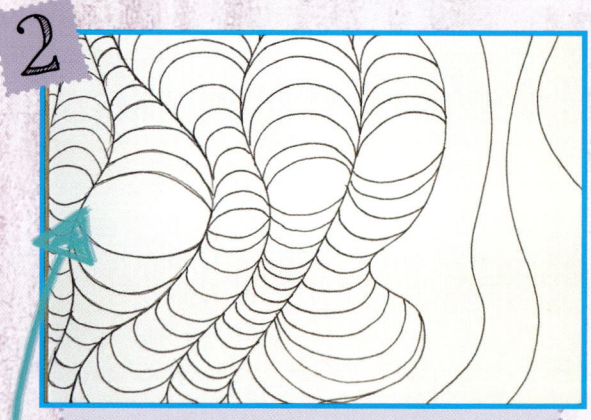

Around halfway down each pair of lines, draw two curves going in opposite directions. Add more arced lines above this point, and add upside-down arcs below.

3

Lightly dip your colored pencil into some lip balm. Use heavy pressure at the sides, and light pressure at the center of each segment.

4

It looks best if you use different shades of the same color for each of your shapes.

Pencil Design

Use your blending skills to draw these colorful pencils.
Try using complementary colors to shade each pencil.
The result looks much nicer than if you just use black.

1

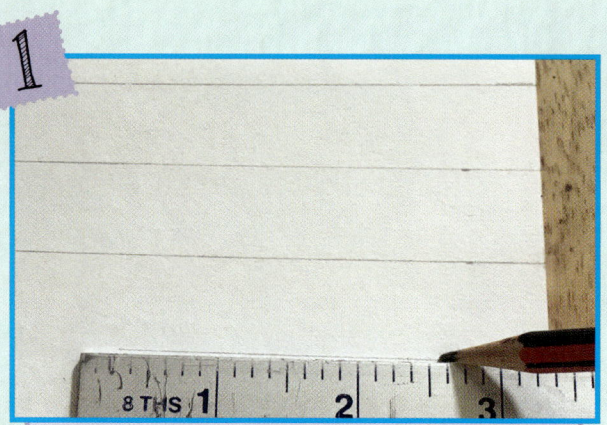

Divide your paper into seven sections with a little space at the top and bottom. Lightly draw the outlines of your seven pencils using a ruler. Make the pencils different lengths.

2

Draw a semicircle at the end of each pair of pencil lines. Then draw a triangle for the wooden point, with a small semicircle at the end.

TIP

Use the side of your colored pencil to shade in large areas. It creates a nice smooth, flat color. Use the point of your pencil for drawing detail, such as the lines in the wooden part of the pencil in step 4.

3

Color your pencils in the seven colors of the rainbow. Press harder to make a darker shade where the pencils meet. Leave a highlight line near the top.

4

Draw some lines in a light brown along the tips, to create a wood effect.

5

Shade any dark areas using each pencil's complementary color. Orange will work for both blues.

Finally, blend each pencil to create a smooth appearance using your white pencil.

Try Colored Paper

In some of the projects already featured in this book, you can see how we've used the white of the paper to be part of our picture. We left the white highlights in our pencils picture, and used the paper color to create highlights in our hand picture. The color of the paper you use can have a big impact on your finished drawing, but it doesn't have to be white!

Master Class

Create Your Own Colored Paper

If you don't have any suitable colored paper, don't worry, it is easy to make your own.

1

2

3

Mix a sandy color using ocher acrylic paint with some water. Using a large brush and even strokes, paint across the paper moving from top to bottom.

To create a sandy texture, quickly scrunch up a tissue and dab the wet surface.

You could also try creating flecks of sand. Once your paint is dry, gently tap a brush full of white or brown paint, while holding it over the paper.

Shells on Sandy Paper

1

Draw a simple arc. Add a toothed edge by drawing an even wavy line all along the arc. Draw the bottom of your shell like the picture above.

2

Draw a faint semicircle at the center bottom of your shell. Draw light lines from each edge of the tooth to the semicircle, to create ridges in the shell.

3

Shade the left-hand side and the left edge of the ridges using purple pencil.

4

Add more shading to your ridges.

Blend over your shell using white pencil.

5

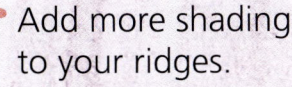

Add blue and purple **horizontal** lines.

21

Bubbles

Using a really dark piece of paper works well with this *bubble* art project. You could use black or dark blue. Creating these *bubbles* is a lot simpler than it looks. Try it.

1

Get some dark paper. Trace around several different-sized round objects using a pencil.

2

Go over each outline using white pencil.

3

Shade the top and bottom edge using two different light colors.

TIP

Drawing a perfect circle can be tricky. A right-handed person will find the top left quarter of a circle the easiest to draw. Instead of struggling, turn the paper around as you trace your outline with white pencil.

4

Using white pencil, draw a rectangle that follows the curve of your circle. Shade one end bright white.

5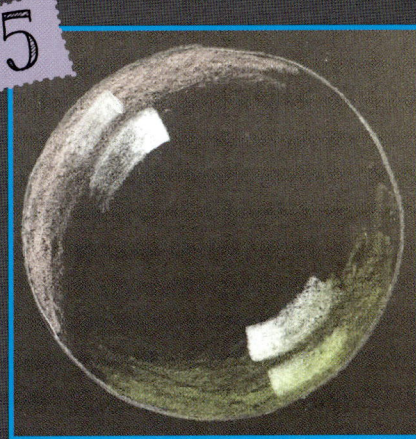

Draw three more similar rectangles. Each one should fade at one end.

6

Add a few more bright colors in some areas around your bubble.

7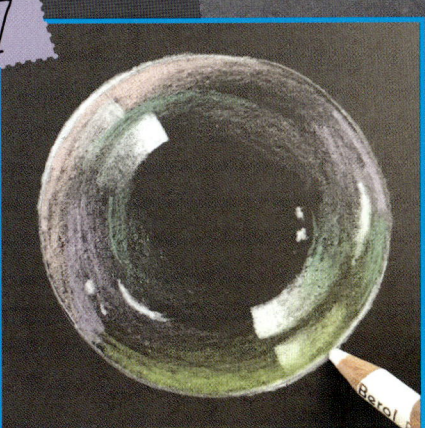

Add a few white dots and curved lines as highlights and your bubble is complete!

Color in your other bubbles in the same way, but using different bright colors.

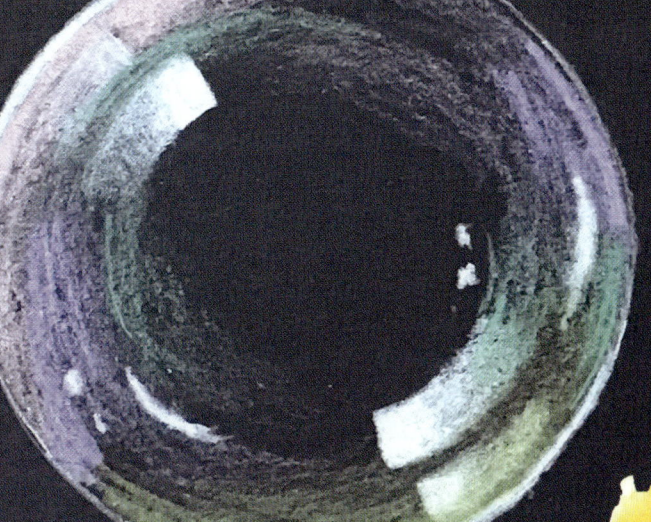

Making an Impression

If you need very fine pale lines in a picture, they can be difficult to keep white as you color the rest of your picture around them. There is a great technique that helps you do this. You simply take a pointed object that is the width of the line you want to create and use it to scratch into the paper. When you color over that area in pencil, the scratch will remain white.

TIP

It is not that easy to see where you have made your marks as you scratch. Try holding your paper at different angles or in different light until you can see the lines that you are drawing.

We used a nail to scratch all the lines, above, into our paper. Then we simply colored over them. If you want to color the lines, you could sharpen a pencil to a fine point and press it into the scratch.

24

The Cat's Whiskers

Try drawing this simple cat with his pure white whiskers.

1

Draw circles for the body and head, and triangle ears. Add a tail.

2

Scratch in the whiskers using a pointed tool.

3

Erase the part of the circle where the tail overlaps.

4

For the fur, draw short lines in the direction the cat's hair would grow.

5

As you add your background, the cat's whiskers will appear like magic!

PROJECT PAGE:
Leaves

Try out your new impression skills and draw these leaves with their delicate veins. Make sure you use white paper if you want the veins to be white.

1

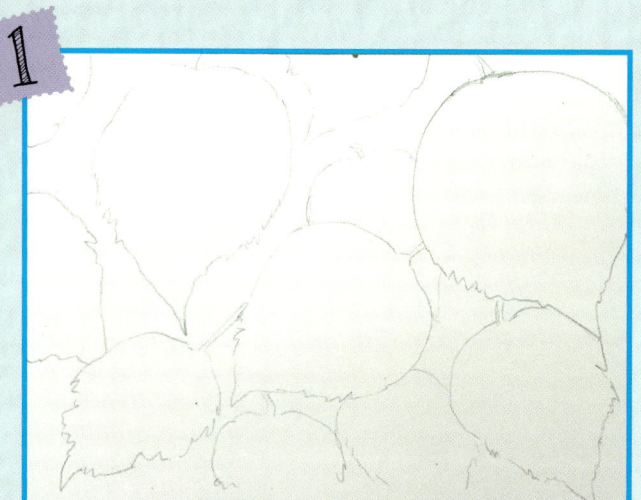

Sketch out a few leaf shapes so they fill your paper. You can make some leaves overlap.

2

Scratch in each leaf's veins using a pointed object. We used a meat skewer this time.

3

Color in around the leaves using dark blue and purple.

TIP

You can add scratches at any point during your drawing. If you wanted yellow veins, you could add some yellow to your leaves first, and then scratch into the color.

Now color in your leaves using the side of a green pencil. Shade the center and edges of each leaf a darker color. Leave some highlights.

You can add darker shading using a blue colored pencil.

Add some yellow to the highlight areas as a finishing touch.

Sled Dog

Try using some of your new techniques to draw this toy dog having fun on his sled. The easiest way to draw the dog is to break him down into simple shapes.

1

Your basic dog shape is made up of two **spheres** for the head and body, and four **cylinders** for the legs. Lightly draw this dog shape near the center of your paper.

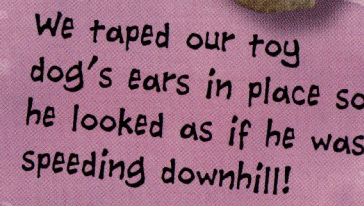
We taped our toy dog's ears in place so he looked as if he was speeding downhill!

2

Add the ears, scarf, and face details to your dog. Copy this sled shape, and draw a simple hill background.

3

Begin coloring in the dog using the scumbling technique. Use two or three different shades of brown to create the fur's highlights and shadows.

4

Draw wavy lines to look like the knitted wool scarf. Go over your lines using light and dark strokes to shade some areas. Use light gray, yellow, or a regular pencil for the white wool's shadows.

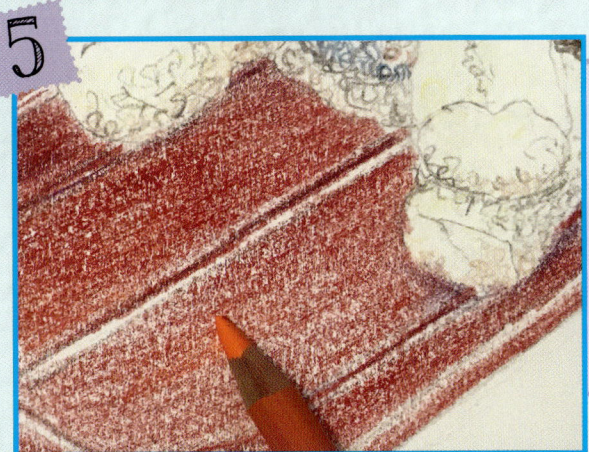

5

Color the sled using red. Brighten the front a little using orange, and put some shadows under and behind the dog using a dark blue. Let the white paper show through where you want strong highlights.

Color your winter sky using light blue, yellow, and gray. Add little patches of gray, blue, and violet to the snow.

Glossary

arc A curved path.

blending Shading into each other.

complementary Colors opposite each other on the color wheel.

contrast To show very noticeable differences.

core A central part of something.

crosshatching Marking with sets of parallel lines that cross.

cylinders Shapes composed of two circular parallel faces of identical size and a curved surface that connects them.

graded Formed a series having only slight differences.

hatching Shading using lines.

highlight The brightest spot or area in a painting or drawing.

horizontal Parallel to the horizon.

layers Many thicknesses of material covering a surface.

optical illusion Something that deceives the eye by appearing to be other than it is.

right angles An angle of 90 degrees, as in a corner of a square.

scumbling Light shading in pencil that gives a soft effect.

shading To mark with changes of light or color.

spheres Globe-shaped bodies.

stippling Applying color by repeated small touches.

texture The structure, feel, and appearance of something.

underpainting The first layer in a painting , indicating the main areas of light and shade.

Further Information

Books

Noble, Marty. *Dover Masterworks: Color Your Own Monet Paintings.* Mineola, NY: Dover Publications, 2013.

Sakamoto, Naoko, and Kamo. *How to Draw Almost Everything for Kids.* Beverly, MA: Quarry Books, 2018.

Websites

Art is Fun website with information about drawing using colored pencils:
www.art-is-fun.com/colored-pencil-art

How to draw a step-by-step landscape using colored pencils:
www.happyfamilyart.com/art-lessons/learn-to-draw/color-pencil-landscape-drawing

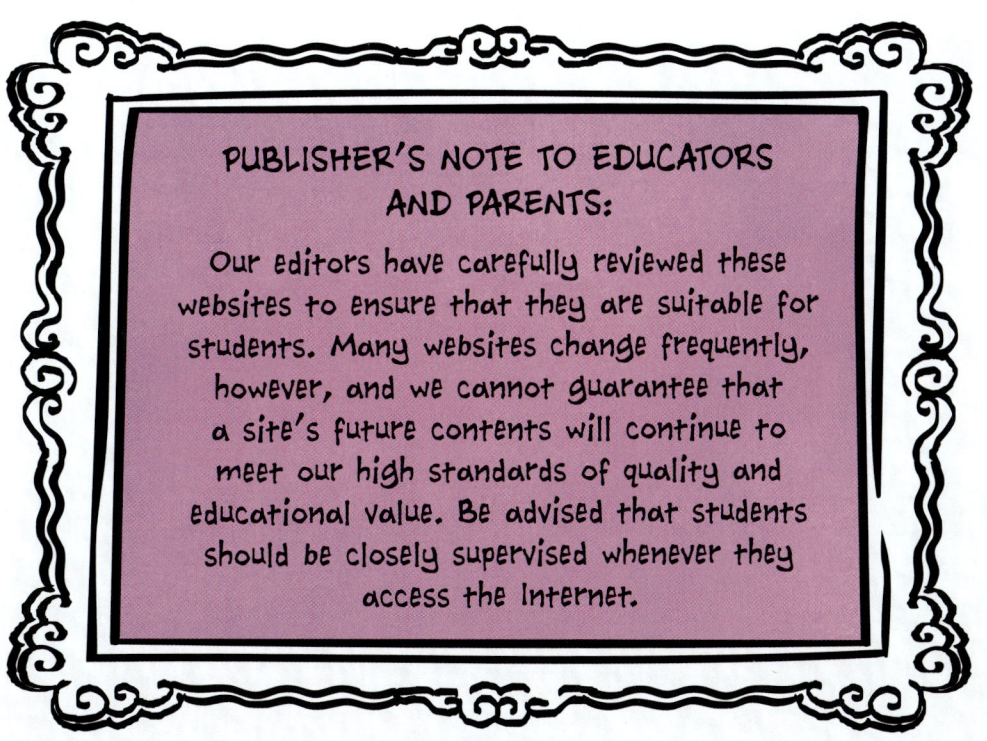

PUBLISHER'S NOTE TO EDUCATORS AND PARENTS:

Our editors have carefully reviewed these websites to ensure that they are suitable for students. Many websites change frequently, however, and we cannot guarantee that a site's future contents will continue to meet our high standards of quality and educational value. Be advised that students should be closely supervised whenever they access the Internet.

Index